THE BOY WHO JUMPED OFF THE TRAIN

MALKA ADLER

Producer & International Distributor
eBookPro Publishing
www.ebook-pro.com

The Boy Who Jumped off the Train
Malka Adler

Copyright © 2022 Malka Adler

All rights reserved; No parts of this book may be reproduced or transmitted in any form or by any means, electronic or mechanical, including photocopying, recording, taping, or by any information retrieval system, without the author's explicit permission in writing.

Illustrations: Jaakov Guterman

Contact: malka.adler@gmail.com
ISBN 9789655752847

*To my parents, Izako and Dora Mitrani,
who embraced grandpa Yitzhak.*

CONTENTS

Tsili, Marishka, and Leah'leh too	7
I'll Pull the Stars out of the Sky for Her	15
Cooking in our Minds	23
The Country's Birthday	37
In a Basement of Suitcases	49
Being Brothers and Friends	57
A Visit to Poland	69
How I Wrote this Story	73

TSILI, MARISHKA & LEAH'LEH TOO

When the summer holidays arrive, I'm happiest of all. My belly even hurts a little I'm so excited. Why? Because I spend the summer holidays with Grandpa Yitzhak and Grandma Hannah, who live on a *Moshav – farm collective.*

Grandpa has a big cowshed with cows and calves, and he lets me feed the calves with a bottle of milk, like a baby's bottle, but much bigger. The calves grab the nipple, suck really fast, and don't let go until it's finished. And we don't have to pick them up for a burp because although they're cow babies, they can already stand by themselves.

I love the quiet on grandpa and grandma's *Moshav*. There are no noisy buses, no cars' hooting. Nobody shouts "Watermelon! Watermelon!" over a loudspeaker. That's because they have a big grocery store nearby that has everything they need.

On the *Moshav* I hear cows mooing, and geese honking

from the neighbor's yard. I also hear a chorus of frogs hiding in the tall grass near the tap. But mostly, the sound of birds. Lots of birds that like to rest in the branches of the big ficus tree that shades the path.

Ah, and the noise of the tractor, but that's maybe only three times a day.

Grandpa Yitzhak loves the cows in the cowshed. He gave each one a girl's name: Tsili, Marishka, Bracha, and Yocheved. I think they're funny names.

I tell grandpa: "Gramps, girls' names are different now, today they have boys' names: Ofir, Daniel, Yuval."

But grandpa laughs and says: "Ittai, names don't change for me."

I tell him, "How come, gramps; how come you aren't on top of things?"

Grandpa says: "I like the old names."

I say: "Why, Gramps? Maybe the cows would prefer new names?"

Grandpa looks at me with grave eyes and says: "When you grow up, you'll understand."

I'm in second grade. I like school. We have sports, like basketball and football. We have computers, make presentations, and we have a special project to do - making a book.

We write short stories on the computer, and then we design a cover, with a title and everything. At the end of the year, we have a big exhibition for all the booklets we prepared during the year. I also like Tamar who sits next to me in class, because she has laughing brown eyes. Tamar has yellow hair that she does up with butterflies that have blue wings.

I finish second grade and, in the first week of the vacation, I go to visit Grandpa and Grandma.

Oh, how happy I am to find three calves in the cowshed that are only two days old. The calves are standing on four little legs and looking at me with curiosity.

I say to grandpa: "Maybe we'll give the sweet little calves new names.

Grandpa says: "What names?"

I say: "Rotem, maybe, or Adi, or Tzvika. I know a girl called Tzvika."

Grandpa sighs and says: "No, no, I already have the names."

"What names?" I ask.

And grandpa says: "The calf with the white mark on her forehead will be Rosie, the calf with the white mark on her knee, Lia, and the third one, Aggie."

I say: "Grandpa, grandpa, where did you find names like those! I've never heard of them!"

Grandpa looks up, frowns, and looks far, far away as if there is an interesting movie he has to see, and he's quiet.

After a few minutes Grandpa gets up and says: "Now I have to go milk the cows."

I go to Grandma Hannah. Grandma has half-moon glasses hanging on a chain over her blouse. She gives me a glass of lemonade made from lemons she picked in the yard, and I say: "Grandma, tell me something, why does Grandpa Yitzhak like names I don't know?"

Grandma says: "Ittai, Grandpa knows the names from Hungary, from places he lived in when he was a boy. But it's a long story, perhaps I'll tell you some other time."

I see that grandma is smiling at me but her eyes are a bit sad.

I say: "Grandma, why are you sad?"

And Grandma says: "Mmm…because of the thoughts in my head. Now, off you go to take a shower."

Evening falls. Grandpa and I are sitting on a bench under the willow tree in the backyard. I look up and see lots and lots of stars shining in the sky. A thin moon sits right above the edge of the cowshed roof. The moon is shaped like a quarter of a grapefruit peel.

I ask grandpa: "How come you have so many stars in the sky here? Do you have a different sky over the *Moshav*?"

Grandpa laughs and puts his arm around me. "No, no," he explains, "there aren't as many lights here as there are in town, it's a full darkness, so the sky is brighter."

I say, "Ah, that's great for you, what a pity we don't see stars." And then I look at grandpa and say quietly, "Grandpa, why do you like names I don't know? And why does Grandma say it's a long story? Won't you tell me?"

Grandpa is quiet.

I'm quiet, too.

Grandpa shakes his head from side to side and sighs: "Oy Marishka, oy Leah'leh, oy Golda'leh, oyoyoy, oyoyoy,"

I look at Grandpa and wait patiently, because I can see on his face that he's thinking a lot of thoughts.

And then Grandpa says: "Well, I'll tell you.

"When I was a boy, Hungary was going through bad times. The Nazis got into power in Germany and declared war on other countries. The Germans occupied Hungary, and they threw us, the Jews, out of our homes. They transported us in trains to a concentration camp and there they separated the families. They sent me, papa Israel, and my older siblings, Sarah, Abraham and Dov to work in labor camps in different places. We had to work very hard. Mama Leah and my grandfather and grandmother, together with all the old people, were left in the concentration camp.

"During the war I met up with my brother, Dov, and after the war, I reunited with my sister, Sarah. Mama, papa and my brother Abraham didn't come back. Neither did grandfather and grandmother. I realized that many boys and girls from my village in Hungary didn't come back either. And this made me very sad.

"Now we live in Israel, our own country, and there are new

names for boys and girls. But I miss the Jewish names I knew in my village in Hungary and I want to remember. That's why I call in the morning: 'Golda, Rivka'leh, Yocheved, good morning!' And at night, I say: 'Marishka, Rosie'leh, good night!"

"I know these names are written in books, but I want to say the names out loud, so that my ears will hear the sound. You, too, my grandson, will hear the names and you'll know that before Rotem and Yuval, children overseas had other names. The little girls with those names had parents and families who loved them very much, just like I love you."

Grandpa takes a handkerchief out of his pocket and wipes his face.

I hug Grandpa.

I don't know why but I feel like calling out loudly: 'Lia, Yocheved, Rivka'leh, Marishka, I love you like grandpa does!'

Instead I whisper, "Night-night, Grandpapa, and thank you for the story."

"Night-night."

I'LL PULL THE STARS OUT OF THE SKY FOR HER

Spring has arrived. Passover is coming and my family and I are going to celebrate *Seder Night - Passover Night*, with Grandpa Yitzhak and Grandma Hannah on the *Moshav*.

We go through the green entrance gate and I can smell the sweet, delicate scent of the citrus trees – orange, lemon, and grapefruit. This scent always reminds me of the holidays.

I see that Grandpa has whitewashed the walls of the house and the stones marking the path to the verandah. He has even whitewashed the trunk of the lemon tree in honor of the holiday.

I get out of the car and run straight to the cowshed, where I find Grandpa, in work clothes complete with high boots. Grandpa is raking a pile of hay, and a strong smell like pickles tickles my nose.

When Grandpa sees me, he puts down the rake.

He says: "Ah, welcome, welcome!" And he hugs me very tight.

My grandpa has very big hands.

I say: "Grandpa Yitzhak, what's new?"

And Grandpa says: "Do you want to meet the new calves?"

I say, "Yes, yes."

And he says, "First, let's welcome our guests."

In the late afternoon, Grandma Hannah sets the table with a white cloth, beautiful dishes and a bottle of wine. Mama helps Grandma and papa works on his lap top because he has a lot to do.

I put on the boots I find in Grandpa's storeroom. He has five pairs of boots. I choose the pair I wore during the summer vacation and I notice that there is less space now between my toes and the end of the boot. I help grandpa feed the cows and spread clean hay next to the trough and when it's time to feed the calves, I give Golda'leh and cute little Hantzi a bottle.

Afterwards we take a shower and put on our holiday clothes. Grandma wears a new apron over her clothes with a large pocket in the shape of an anemone.

We sit down at the table and I see that there's an empty chair next to grandpa.

I say: "What's that, Gramps, a chair for Elijah the Prophet?"

Grandpa smiles at me and says: "No, Ittai, the chair is not for Elijah the Prophet."

I ask: "So who is the empty chair for? Do you have a guest who's stuck in traffic?"

Grandpa laughs, saying: "No, no, the chair is for a girl."

I sit up in my chair and ask, "What girl? Where is she? Do I know her?"

Grandpa straightens the chair under the table cloth and laughs: "Maybe she'll come, my girl, maybe."

"What will she come for?" I ask, looking at Grandma Hannah.

Grandpa says: "I need to thank her for everything."

Standing up, I say: "What do you need to thank her for, Gramps?"

Grandpa caresses the empty chair and says: "It's a long story. We'll read first."

We read the *Haggadah - the Story of the Exodus*, and sing songs. I taste some of the red wine and easily find the *Afikoman* - a small piece of Matzo, traditionally hidden for kids to find and be rewarded.

Afterwards we eat the good food that Grandma prepared and I eat quickly because I'm curious and want to hear Grandpa's story about this mysterious girl.

After the meal I go out to the backyard with Grandpa. We sit down on the swinging bench under the big willow tree and I say: "Gramps, tell me about the girl you want to thank. Will you?"

Grandpa sighs: "Well, I'll tell you.

Do you remember me telling you about when I was a boy in Hungary? The Nazis came to power in Germany and declared war on other countries. The Germans occupied Hungary and threw us, the Jews, out of their homes. They broke up my family, sending us all to different places and I was sent to a special work camp in Germany.

"Every morning I would set out on foot in a convoy to work in a large factory. I had to wrap special material around steel pipes. At first, because it was summer, the weather was quite pleasant. But after a while, winter came, it rained and there were fierce snow storms. The clothes I was wearing were suitable for summer, not winter. They looked like striped pajamas. My body ached with cold.

"At the labor camp we were given very little food. I was hungry and sad because I missed my family."

"How old were you, Gramps?"

"Fifteen and a few months."

"Couldn't you go home?"

"No, we were prisoners. Armed guards watched us.

One day, at dawn, I'm walking in the convoy. The sky is

gray and very cold and I can hear my belly rumbling with hunger. The convoy nears a German village not far from the road we're walking along. I progress slowly and, in the distance, I see two figures at the side of the road. One is tall, and one almost my height. They look like mother and daughter.

"We approach them. I see that the girl is holding a parcel in her hands. The mother signals the German soldier to stop. We stop. The girl looks at me and whispers in her mother's ear. The mother goes over to the guard, speaks to him in German and points to me. My heart starts pounding quickly. I don't understand what's going on. I see the guard nod his head. The girl approaches me, gives me the parcel and immediately walks away. I don't know what to do. The guard tells me to open it. I open it. In the parcel is a large sausage sandwich. I swallow the sandwich with one bite. The guard motions to the convoy to start walking. I feel as if I've been given the strength to go on.

"That night I couldn't fall asleep with excitement. I didn't understand why the girl chose to give *me* the sandwich.

"The next day the mother and daughter were standing next to the road again. The girl was holding a parcel. Our convoy stopped next to the two. I thought I'd faint with excitement. The girl gave me the parcel. I found cooked carrot and potato. The adult prisoners wanted to grab the food from me, but the German guard wouldn't allow them to come near me.

"The German girl and her mother waited for my convoy for weeks. When snow began to fall, they disappeared and I never saw them again.

"I don't know the name of the girl. I didn't speak to her because it was forbidden for a Jewish prisoner to talk to Germans. I know she saved me from starvation. The food she brought me gave me the strength to get through the hard period in the labor camp. And the smile, too."

I ask: "What smile?"

Grandpa says: "The girl had blue eyes and she smiled at me. In those days, a small smile was as important as a sandwich. I remember trying not to cry."

"Why, Gramps?"

"Because I was alone, alone among strangers, and from morning till night all I heard were shouts and curses. Do you know how happy it made me to discover there was one girl in the world who cared about me?"

Grandpa looks at me. "That's why, every Passover, I set out an empty chair for her. I think, maybe she'll come and I'll finally be able to say thank you. And if she comes I'll make her a queen and I'll pull the stars out of the sky for her, I…… Aah."

I hug Grandpa. I see he has tears in his eyes. I run to the kitchen to fetch him a glass of juice. Grandpa drinks the juice and I say: "What a pity the German girl hasn't come, I'd like to meet her.

Grandpa sighs and says: "Well, you met her through the story. I often think about her and I know that there can be good people even in the most evil of places. Sometimes we have to look for them, but we can always find them, we only have to believe they exist."

COOKING IN OUR MINDS

It wasn't only Grandpa Yitzhak who told thrilling stories. My classmate, Tamar, has a grandma who also has stories to tell. Her grandma's name is Sida. A few months ago, during *Hannukah – Festival of lights* – Tamar invited me to go with her to visit her grandmother.

We travel by train. On the way, Tamar tells me about her grandmother.

"My Grandma Sida's home is the sweetest in the world. When we go to Grandma Sida, the first thing we always do is go into the kitchen. The entrance door leads straight to a small dining table and four chairs, and even if we aren't hungry, we sit down to eat.

"Grandma Sida's food tastes really good. And I always finish my plate quickly because I love her dessert best of all: swiss roll, crisp brownies, blintzes with raisins and jam, and cookies with sesame seeds that we make together.

"From the kitchen we go into the bedroom. I get undressed, put on my festive pajamas with ruffles and ribbons, and I'm invited to sit in her big bed and listen to stories. Grandma's bed is on wheels and you can lie in it and push with your feet. The bed rolls up to the opposite wall and back again, it's so much fun. While the bed rolls, Grandma Sida takes a fancy box of chocolates out of the drawer. I sit up at once, suck a chocolate, and Grandma reads funny stories to me from a book with tiny print.

"If I sleep over at Grandma's on a school night, she sends me off to school in the morning with a full bag of food – sandwiches, fruit, waffles, cookies – enough for at least five children. I always tell her, 'Grandy, it's too much food for me, please, take some out'. But Grandma won't hear of it. 'No and no, sweetheart, you might need it', I take it all and share it with my friends because she's taught me that we mustn't throw away food, or give it back. 'There are a lot of hungry children in the world,' she always says, 'so you must finish what's on your plate and say thank you.'"

I tell Tamar: "At Grandpa Yitzhak's, too, it's forbidden to throw away food. Sometimes I eat and I'm already full and leave a small piece of pita. Grandpa doesn't throw it out. He puts the pita on a plate for later."

Tamar says: "A little piece of bread, too, right?"

I say: "Even a slice of orange."

Tamar says: "I told you they're alike."

We reach Grandma Sida and I give her a bunch of chrysanthemums wrapped in cellophane. Grandma thanks me and immediately puts the flowers into a glass vase. I notice she adds a teaspoon of sugar.

She smiles and says, "it helps the flowers last longer."

Tamar gives Grandma a clay *Menorah – special Passover candlesticks* - that she made in a ceramics class at school. Grandma marvels at the artwork, saying: "We'll light two Menorahs this evening, yours and mine."

Tamar says: "You know, Ittai, my grandma is very attached to her Menorah. It's silver with a large Magen David where the *Shamash – the helper candle* hangs. She found it many years ago in a little store in Tel Aviv. She told me that the Menorah reminds her of her home overseas, which she had to leave during the war. She doesn't have any keepsakes from home. No objects or photograph albums."

Grandma Sida sighs and says: "That's enough now, let's eat."

We wash our hands, and immediately receive a plate filled with meatballs and stuffed peppers. We eat fast and have thick 'bird' milk for dessert that she cooked in a pot. Mmm, very tasty.

I ask Grandma Sida: "Bird milk? How did you make it?"

And she tells me: "Two glasses of milk, vanilla essence, six eggs, fine sugar, and a little cornflower. We used to call it bird milk at home." Then she promises: "I'll tell you how to cook it another time, all right?"

After the meal, Grandma Sida and Tamar put on long aprons down to their knees and, out of the cupboard, Grandma takes a large bowl covered with a towel. I peep under the towel and see dough that has risen nicely. Grandma carefully removes the towel, and the two pull off small pieces of dough, and fry plump donuts in deep, boiling oil. We hear tsssss, tsssss, like cymbals rubbing together and the house fills with a sweet smell.

I arrange the brown donuts on absorbent paper on a tray, and once they're fried I sprinkle powdered sugar on top. And I'm happy, oh how happy I am, even the warm donuts are smiling.

Evening falls.

We light the first candle on each Menorah, sing Hannukah songs and eat donuts that *gritz gritz* in the mouth. After three donuts, our bellies are almost bursting, but Grandma pleads with us:

"Eat, my sweethearts, eat more, more, and may you never lack for food, because hunger is a terrible thing."

Tamar and I look at each other.

Tamar says: "But Grandma, there's no way we'd be hungry in your home, we have food even when we're full."

Grandma sighs and says: "True, but I've known other days, it's better not to talk about it."

Grandma washes the dishes in the sink, I dry the glasses and Tamar arranges them in the cupboard. We don't talk, but my head is full of thoughts: Grandpa Yitzhak talks about other days, too, and his face suddenly gets serious, just like Grandma Sida. Maybe they were in the same place? And maybe there's a story coming?

My heart starts beating fast, I look at Tamar, she gestures to me to be quiet. I hurriedly dry the cutlery, thinking, I hope so, I hope so.

It's time for bed. We're in Grandma Sida's large bed. She picks up the book of funny stories and Tamar puts her hand on it.

Tamar says quietly: "Grandma, won't you tell us about the other days you knew, please."

Grandma says: "No, no, only funny stories before bed."

And I ask myself, does Tamar's grandma only have sad stories, too?

Tamar purses her lips. Grandma Sida glances at her and turns on a small radio that's always on the side table.

Tamar says to Grandma: "Why is the radio always on at night? After all, we're fast asleep!"

Grandma clears her throat and says: "The radio is on in case I wake during the night. I like to hear sounds."

I ask: "Why do you like to hear sounds in the middle of the night?"

Grandma bites her lips and says quietly: "So that I know I'm alive."

I don't understand, and I'm a little scared, and Grandma says: "Ittai, I see by your forehead that you have a lot of questions. We'll put it off until tomorrow, all right? Now we'll read the book."

I lie on one side of Grandma, Tamar on the other. I hear Tamar whisper in her ear, "Grandy, tickle me."

A tickle for them means stroking your arm. Grandma gently strokes from top to bottom, and back again, slowly, slowly, and reads the story.

And then she says: "Ittai would you also like a tickle along your arm?"

We laugh.

The next day, the three of us are sitting on a bench in the park. I see small children playing with a puppy, and two adults reading a newspaper. Tamar looks into her grandmother's beautiful face and says: "I really want to hear about those other days overseas, you promised, remember?"

I add: "Grandma Sida, do you know that my grandfather tells me stories about his childhood overseas? He was in the war. I really like hearing his stories."

Grandma takes a deep breath, and says: "Really Ittai? I wonder where your Grandpa was."

And then she sighs and says: "Maybe it really is time."

She straightens her dress over her knees and starts to speak: "I was born in Slovakia in Europe, in a town called Topoľčany. In our town there were perhaps three thousand Jews. I was my parents' eldest daughter and I had three little brothers. We had a good life in Topoľčany. Mama and Papa worked, my brothers and I went to school, except for our little brother who was five years old.

"And then the war started in Europe. The Germans occupied Slovakia and drove the Jews from their homes and sent them to a transit camp. We spent three weeks there and the day after Yom Kippur, they took me, Mama, and my three brothers by train to a concentration camp in Poland. Papa remained in the transit camp because he had work there in the kitchen.

"The moment we got off the train, the Germans separated me from my family. I saw my mother walking away with my three brothers. She held my youngest brother's hand. I was sent to a labor camp in Germany. I was sixteen and I was alone.

"At the camp in Germany, I worked at a turnery in an airplane factory. Twelve hours a day on my feet. We made bearings. Those are the metal parts that enable a wheel to turn. Before we started work they gave us a special course.

"There were hundreds of women and girls in the camp. The German guards divided us into groups, and we worked either day or night shifts. I worked the night shift, and we only went to sleep in the morning. We were twenty girls to a room and had separate beds. We were given a little food – a quarter of a loaf of bread per day, sometimes less, and thin soup. It wasn't enough. We were so hungry, we started cooking in our minds."

Tamar asks, "what does 'cooking in our minds' mean?"

Grandma explains: "Because of the terrible hunger, we didn't stop talking about food. Mainly on a Sunday, when we didn't work. We'd sit in the room and recall the food we knew how to cook at home, and we started exchanging recipes.

"I was an expert on thin noodles prepared out of dough. I'd spread dough on the table, stretching it with a rolling pin, like a table cloth, and divide it into quarters. I'd roll out each quarter like a roulade. Then I'd cut small strips with a knife, and make fine noodles like the ones you can buy today in packets.

"There were girls who taught us to cook *palačinka*, - blintzes, and *turosh delkli* which is a sweet yeast dough. One of them taught us to make *rakott krumpli*, layers of potato and eggs, a meal I prepare to this day, and everyone enjoys it, right sweetheart?"

Tamar says: "Yes, grandma, I like *rakott krumpli* very much."

Grandma continues: "When we exchanged recipes, we also talked about home. We talked about our families, and recalled prayers and songs we'd sing on the holidays. Sometimes we'd sing quietly, and it made us strong and gave us hope."

Tamar asks Grandma: "Where did you learn to cook so young?"

Grandma says: "A few years before we were expelled from the town, we Jews were forbidden to employ maids. Mama said we children had to share the work. I wasn't any good at cleaning, every time I washed the floor, Mama would go over it again with a rag. So she put me in the kitchen and said, 'you will cook.' And she taught me. I actually enjoyed cooking. Every Friday, I'd prepare a large amount of sweet dough. From this I'd make *Challot – Sabbath bread* – yeast cake with cheese filling, and cakes with cocoa. And the Shabbat delicacy was a glass of cocoa. Oh, how I loved drinking cocoa."

Tamar asks: "Grandma how did you manage in the labor camp with only a piece of bread when you were used to eating good food?"

And Grandma replies: "The hunger was hard, very hard, but we had tricks."

"What tricks?" I ask.

"Well," says Grandma, "on Sundays we were allowed to fetch hot water from the kitchen. Every time, two girls would take buckets to the kitchen to fill up with water. In the kitchen was a huge sack of powder, like a soup mix. The Germans forbade us to take this powder. We didn't listen to them. While we were in the kitchen, with one hand we'd hold the bucket and with the other we'd put a handful of powder in our pockets. We called it *chicchirichi*. We had a heating stove on the bloc. We'd put the powder in the bucket, which we'd then put on the stove until it boiled, and so every Sunday we had a quarter of a loaf of bread with *chicchirichi* soup we made for ourselves."

Tamar asks: "Was that enough for all of you?"

Grandma says: "No, sweetheart. We were always hungry in the camp. But it gave us a little flavor. Because of the hunger, we lost a lot of weight, and we were always afraid we wouldn't have the strength to get up in the morning for work. Women who were too weak to get up in the morning or who were ill, disappeared from the camp. So we did everything we could to find food."

I ask: "How did you find food, Grandma Sida?"

And Grandma answers: "In all kinds of ways. For instance,

when we went out at night to work, we walked along the railway track. We walked for an hour – summer and winter, it made no difference. As we walked, we always looked for food next to the track. Sometimes we'd find turnip or potato peels, or even an apple peel thrown out of the train. Potato peels were a real treat for us.

"I remember one time in particular. I was the last in the group of girls who went to get food for everyone. We carried heavy jars of soup. At the bottom of the jar was a tiny piece of something solid, vegetables perhaps, or meat, I don't know. Solid food was considered the best, because it filled the belly a bit.

"We were walking with the jars when the German guard suddenly yelled: 'Stop!" We stopped. The guard walked off. Maybe he had to pee. I quickly opened the lid of the jar and peeped inside. I saw the soup was very hot. And I took off my shoe – we had shoes like wooden Dutch clogs – and I quickly pushed the shoe inside the jar. I filled it with soup and some pieces and took a huge mouthful, even though it

was boiling. I didn't have time for more than a mouthful, because the German guard came back." Tamar and I cried out: "Boiling soup"?

Grandma says: "Yes, my sweethearts, it was hard, very hard, but we wanted to live."

Grandma frowns and says quietly: "At the end of the war, I swore, yes, I swore that my home would never lack for food."

And then she turns to Tamar and says: "Now do you understand?"

Tamar hugs Grandma. I also hug her. She pats us gently on the back and says, "Come on, time to eat."

"But I'm not hungry," Tamar tells Grandma.

To which Grandma Sida replies: "My belly isn't hungry either, but my mind, my mind, sweetheart, that's another story."

THE COUNTRY'S BIRTHDAY

As Independence Day approaches, Grandpa Yitzhak telephones me and says: "Ittai my boy, I want you to be our guest on Independence Day. There'll be a big party on the *Moshav* and you should come. Will you?

I jump up and down and let out a sharp whistle. Grandpa laughs and says, "Got it. So, I'll see you for the holiday."

I run to Mama, calling: "Grandpa's invited me for the holiday! Grandpa invited me! Can I go?"

Mama says: "We thought we'd go on a picnic with friends in one of the forests. Do you want to go to Grandpa and Grandma?"

I nod and say: "Yes, yes, yes."

"But your friends will be at the picnic, Stav, Omer and Roee. Think about it, maybe?" says Mama.

"Grandpa is also my friend, and I prefer to be with him," I say, knowing in my heart that it's because of his stories.

On Independence Day I get down from the bus near Grandpa's *Moshav* and see the Israeli flag hanging from the top of the water tower down to the ground. Wow, I think to myself, the tower is as high as a three-story building, how many rolls of fabric did they need to reach that length?

I raise my left hand, stretch it out in front of me, close one eye, and start measuring the flag with my fingers. One, two, three, four, five… I'm almost at the middle of the flag, when a jarring bzzzzz sounds near my ear. I turn to my right and see a large bee flying around me.

Standing quite still, I follow the bee with my eyes. Grandpa taught me to wait quietly until the bee goes away, because a bee sting is very painful.

The bee vanishes and I start measuring again…ten, eleven, twelve, thirteen, and fourteen, ugh, enough.

Picking up my bag from the sidewalk, I start walking in the direction of Grandma and Grandpa's house. Along the road are bougainvillea bushes in bright colors, red, purple, pink and white. A small bee travels towards and then floats way above the tall bushes. Suddenly she lands on a heavy bunch of flowers and vanishes inside.

At the entrance to Grandpa's yard I suddenly stand still and look around. What, am I mistaken? Is this the yard?

Yes. No. Yes. Yes? Wait…

"Why, of course it is," I say aloud, this is the yard, this is the house. For a moment I was confused by all the flags. And what flags!

An Israeli flag is flying from the roof of the house. Another from the roof of the cowshed. Medium-sized flags are stuck in the potted plants on the verandah, and the fence posts next to the cowshed are also decorated. Hanging between the trees in the yard are small chains of plastic flags like a birthday celebration, and I hear the song *'Here, I was born; here, I built my home'* filling the yard.

I run in the direction of the cowshed and Grandpa Yitzhak comes out to greet me.

I receive a big hug and cry out: "Yo, Gramps, this is great! For a moment, I thought I was in the Kfar Saba Mall carpark. It's how we decorate for Independence Day."

Grandpa high-fives me, turns on the spot and says: "Well, do you think it's beautiful?"

I cry out: "Very beautiful, like a birthday."

Grandpa says: "Of course, today is our country's birthday, isn't it? And for me, it's the most important birthday, d'ya understand?"

I ask: "More important than yours and Grandmas birthdays?"

Grandpa bends down and says: "Remember what I say, boy. It's the most important of all, of all. Is that clear?"

I see Grandpa's face is getting serious, and my heart starts to jump in my chest. Because I know that look of his. It's how he looks when he's remembering things. Oh, how I love Grandpa's stories, even more than the stories in the books I borrow from the library.

I glance in the direction of the swing in the backyard.

Grandpa nods and says: "First we'll go in to Grandma, she's prepared goodies for you."

It's afternoon. Grandpa and I are sitting under the willow tree. Grandpa is staring at the flag flying on the roof of the house, and his lips are moving as if he is whispering. He starts tapping his fingers on the wooden bench, tok, tok. Tok-tok-tok, and slowly he gets into the rhythm, accompanying himself as he sings aloud: *"To be a free nation in our country, land of Zion and Jerusalem."*

I say: "Gramps, gramps, you're singing a line from our anthem! Are you going to sing solo at the *Moshav* party?"

Grandpa looks at me with huge eyes and says, "no, my boy, I'm not planning to sing at the party."

"So why are you singing especially now?" I ask.

Grandpa says: "Because I'm especially happy today. The Independence Day holiday is my favorite holiday of the year."

I ask: "More than... Hannukah, for instance?"

And he says: "Look around you. Don't you see the

happiness in my yard? The branches of the trees are swaying gently and tugging at the chains of flags as if they were dancing. And the tiles on the roof, showing off the flag flying above them, can't you see they seem to have red cheeks? Even the fence posts near the cowshed are several centimeters taller because of the decorations, am I right or not?"

Looking around I say: "It's truly a festive yard."

And Grandpa says: "And why is that, my grandson? Well, what do you say?"

Without waiting for a reply, he goes on: "Because I'm happy and proud to live in the State of Israel, which is my country. You, sweetheart, were born in Israel, maybe it's hard for you to understand."

"What's hard for me to understand, Grandpa?"

"Do you remember I told you about the hard times I went through in my childhood, during the Second World War? In those days, Jews didn't have a country. We lived in a village in Hungary, maybe six hundred families, of which thirty were Jewish families. One day, the Nazis who were in control of Germany, began to expel us from our homes. Look at the house, boy, a big house, full of furniture, and dishes, curtains, pictures and books. Look at the cowshed, with its cows and calves we have to feed. Imagine foreign soldiers coming and giving orders: All of you have to leave the village! You have one hour."

I say: "Why would they say something like that?"
And Grandpa says: "I didn't understand why we had to leave our home either. We were born in that village, we went to school there, we played with our friends there. The gentiles went to pray in church, and we Jews went to pray in the synagogue. We didn't bother them, quite the opposite, we helped each other whenever needed . We even celebrated family events together. And suddenly, Hungarian soldiers

are giving the order: "The Jews have to get out! That's it."

Grandpa sighs and continues: "How do you pack up a home in one hour? What do you take, what do you leave behind? How long will we stay in the new place, and where will we go? Who will feed and milk the cows in the cowshed? Who will take care of the chickens and the geese in the yard?

We had no answer.

"One hour! That's what they told Papa in the synagogue. He went that morning to pray, because it was a holiday, the day after Passover. At first, we didn't want to listen to Papa, my brothers and I shouted: 'What do you mean, pack up? The war is over. We can hear the sounds of Russian canon in the distance.'

It didn't help.

"I remember Mama wanting to wash the Passover dishes and put them away in the cupboard. She didn't have time."

I bite my lips and say: "What did you do, Gramps, what?"

Grandpa says: "We grabbed some clothes and blankets, holy books and some plates, and we tied them up in sheets. Because we didn't have bags or suitcases. Understand, my grandson, we'd never left that village. Only for brief trips, like going to the nearby town market, or to family who lived in villages not far from us."

I plea: "Gramps I don't understand, couldn't you oppose the expulsion."

And Grandpa shouts: "No! Hungarian soldiers were standing near our home. They had guns!"

Then he goes on: "We left home on Passover. We spent a month in a transit camp. We slept under the open sky, in the rain and mud. They brought thousands of Jews from all the cities and nearby villages to that camp. And then they sent us by train to Poland. We arrived at a huge camp at night, and there I lost my family."

I stroke Grandpa's hand and feel like yelling: 'Why? Why? Why?'

I remain silent.

Grandpa continues: "I remained in Poland for several weeks and I saw hundreds of trains filled with Jews arriving at the camp. Maybe even thousands. The Nazis didn't only drive Jews out of Hungary. They drove Jews out of many countries in Europe. I knew that a terrible disaster had befallen my people, and there was nothing I could do. Nothing. My heart wept.

"After the war, I returned to my village in Hungary. I was the only one to return. Villagers I didn't know were living in our house. Their children were wearing clothes that belonged to me and my brother Dov. When I walked along the path and introduced myself, the farmer was astonished to see me. He was sure none of my family would return. He said, 'by the pictures in the newspapers, we thought there were no Jews left in the world.' And then he whispered to me, 'You should leave, there are no more Jews here. You don't belong here.'

I heard the farmer and felt great rage. I told him, 'you are greatly mistaken, sir. I am a Jew and I have returned.'

"I didn't remain in the village. Not because of what the farmer said. I didn't want to stay because at the end of the war I swore I'd only live among Jews in *Eretz Israel*. So that no-one would ever drive me out of my home again. Yes.

"I traveled with my brother Dov to *Eretz Israel*. It was two years before the establishment of the State. At first, we were sent to a *Moshav* in the Galilee to work and learn Hebrew. But I wanted to be a soldier. A soldier with a gun who could protect his home.

"I became a soldier who accompanied convoys. I had a gun and I brought food in a backpack for my heroic friends on Kibbutz Yehi'am. When I held my rifle, my eyes grew moist, you know why? Because I, Yitzhak son of Leah and Israel of blessed memory, didn't believe I'd ever hold a gun in my hands. Hungarians had guns. Germans had guns. And what did I have – nothing. And here I am, three years later, and I have a country. I was a proud Jew in my country, a free Jew."

Grandpa fell silent. I see that his forehead is wet. His eyes too. I grab his hand and say quietly: "That's why you love to

sing 'be a free people in our country'…"

"Yes", says Grandpa, straightening his neck. "If I'm safe in my country, I'm a happy man."

I stroke Grandpa's hand and he leans back. A few minutes go by and then he says: "Forgive me, my boy, I got a little upset. What's your favorite holiday?"

I think for a moment and say: "I love Hannukah."

"And why is that?" asks Grandpa.

"Because you can find jam donuts in the stores two months before the holiday, and I love donuts."

"Ah," says Grandpa, "and what about Purim? Don't the stores in Kfar Saba sell *Hamantaschen – special Purim biscuits?*

I say: "They do, they do, but you also have to come up with a fancy-dress costume to wear, and I don't really like wearing a costume on Purim. Hannukah's better."

Grandpa says: "Ittai, my boy, the most important thing is that you can celebrate all the Jewish holidays in your country, even if you don't like dressing up on Purim, right?"

I nod and smell potato latkes. My nose starts itching and Grandpa says: "Ah? You miss them? So, let's go in to the kitchen, because Grandma Hannah has made potato latkes in your honor, especially for Independence Day."

I hold Grandpa's hand and say, "Gramps, I really love the stories you tell me. Do you have another one for me?"

Grandpa ruffles my hair and says: "Right now, we're going to eat latkes. This evening we'll go to a party, maybe… tomorrow."

Yes, tomorrow, tomorrow. Oh, my gramps.

IN A BASEMENT OF SUITCASES

The next day comes.

Grandpa and I are sitting on the story bench and Grandpa asks: "Well, did you enjoy our party yesterday?"

I say: "I enjoyed it very much."

Grandpa says: "What did you enjoy most?"

I say: "The boy band. Particularly the drummer. Did you see how he managed to play on all those drums, and the cymbals. He even knows how to play the conga drums!"

Grandpa replies: "We're very proud of our boys' band, they're all talented. But I like folk dancing most of all. Did you see the girls with their flying dresses jumping into the air, and the boys with their embroidered shirts, holding out their arms, hop to catch them? Sometimes I'm afraid that one of the girls will fall and break an arm or a leg. High jumps are risky."

I say: "Trust them, Gramps, they're professionals."

And Grandpa says: "It's still frightening, I know!"

"How do you know," I ask. "Did you do folk dancing in couples?"

Grandpa laughs and says: "No, no, I've never danced. I barely agree to dance the tango at weddings, but your grandmother insists. But jumping up high is scary."

I look at Grandpa and see his eyes half closed, a sign that he's remembering something.

I wait patiently.

Grandpa pushes his foot against the ground and the bench starts to swing, forwards and backwards. Forwards and backwards. And then he presses down his foot as if he's pressing on breaks, and we stop. He says, "I don't know if I've told you, but during the war we marched on foot and we traveled on trains. There were instances when during the train journey the skies caught fire. American and British airplanes would see a German train and immediately bomb it. The pilots didn't know that there were prisoners on those trains.

"When the bombs started, the train stopped and the German guards would jump down to take shelter. They forbade us to jump, because they didn't care about us. The plight of the prisoners was of no interest to them and even when some of us were wounded, they didn't help."

I ask: "So what did you do, Gramps? Did you have anywhere to hide on the train?"

Grandpa said: "No, Ittai, there was no hiding place. The trains were open even if it was snowing. But we didn't listen to them. The moment the bombing started, we jumped down after them. We jumped down to look for food. The bombing didn't bother us, it was the hunger that was hard.

"One day, the train entered a station in one of the German cities. It was snowing. I heard the wailing of planes and the thwack of a machine gun. We immediately jumped down from the car and ran like hungry rats in search of food. We ran from door to door, building to building. We found nothing. And then we came to the window of a rather dark basement the size of two rooms. The basement floor was filled with closed suitcases. The window was narrow and barred. I stood at the window with several other adult prisoners, and I saw them looking at me. I realized they wanted me to go down into the basement to look for food for everyone. Because I was the smallest and thinnest, I was the only one who could pass through the bars."

I interrupt: "But weren't you afraid to jump down alone into the basement?" "

"I didn't think about it," says Grandpa, adding: "The possibility of finding food was my whole focus. I grabbed the bars and put my leg inside, and then I slipped my whole body through. I hung in the air, one, two, three, and hop, I jumped. I landed on a fat brown suitcase. I quickly opened

it. I shook out clothes, threw out silver dishes, books, pictures, sweaters, slippers, but no food.

"I opened another suitcase. I looked in coat pockets, checked the sides, and didn't find a thing. I emptied a third suitcase, a fourth, a fifth. The prisoners kept watch for me from above. They didn't say a word. I overturned dozens of suitcases. Nothing.

"I wanted to get out."

"I looked up and saw that the distance from the floor to the window seemed very scary. Distance sometimes seems bigger when you're looking from the floor upwards, you know that?"

I say: "Yes, of course I know that. So, what did you do?"

"The prisoner above called to me, 'Put one suitcase on top of another and climb up.' The prisoner had a voice like my father's. The voice of someone who knows things.

"I threw some clothes into several suitcases, closed them quickly and positioned them like a tower. I climbed up the pile. The suitcases sank under my feet, and I fell down. The prisoner shouted to me: 'The bombing has stopped, hurry!' I felt as if my legs were melting like butter in the sun. I looked for items that were hard and pushed books and silver plates into the suitcases on top of the clothes. I positioned a taller pile. I climbed up carefully, my body swayed, my legs were trembling; I slowly stood up and raised my head. I heard the voice like my father's again saying: 'Yitzhak, jump, jump!' I saw thin hands coming down towards me through the bars. I lifted my hands very, very slowly. I was too far away, I took a deep breath and jumped. Once more, I fell to the floor."

I jump up and call out: "Oh, gramps, gramps, how will you get out of that cellar!"

Grandpa sits me down and says: "Patience, you'll see.

Suddenly, I heard a train whistle. I was afraid that the prisoners would run to the train and leave me alone. Looking up I screamed to them: 'Help me get out! I have to get out of here!' I beat myself on the head and shouted: 'Yitzhak, think! Think! Otherwise, you'll be left here among the suitcases.'

"The voice of the prisoner who sounded like my father called from above: 'Go back to the suitcases. Try, quickly, a guard is coming, I'm waiting for you!'

"I felt stronger, I took a deep breath. I wiped my moist hands on my shirt, I looked for the biggest suitcases in the pile. I put them one on top of the other in a straight line. I climbed up carefully, straightening up slowly. I barely moved. I heard: "Yitzhak, jump! Jump!" I slightly bent my knees, and jumped upward, towards the bars. Two hands firmly caught me. I heard the sound like my father's voice breathing above me: 'hold tight! Hold on, I'm pulling you up!' Several hands caught me, and they pulled and pulled. I pushed my feet against the wall and reached the bars. I was out. And then I saw a German guard approaching me. I ran fast to the nearest car and fell onto the straw."

Throwing myself on Grandpa, I hug him fiercely. I say: "Oh Gramps, I was so afraid, how lucky you were to get out of there."

Grandpa closes his eyes.

I want to cry but stop myself. I say: "Grandpa, are you tired?"

Grandpa says quietly: "No, sweetheart, just a bit upset."

I ask: "Did you meet the man who saved you?"

Grandpa replies: "He ran to another car. We didn't meet again. To this day I can hear his voice in my ears, 'Yitzhak, jump! Jump!!' Some things you never forget."

The sky fills with stars. A full moon rises gradually above the cowshed roof.

I get down quickly from the bench and start gently rocking Grandpa. Grandpa smiles with closed eyes and hums a tune: *"Every night the wind blows, every night the treetops rustle..."*

I join in quietly until Grandpa falls asleep.

BEING BROTHERS AND FRIENDS

I finish third grade. The summer vacation arrives and I go, as always, to visit Grandpa Yitzhak and Grandma Hannah who live on a *Moshav*. During the journey, I look out of the car window and see that the green fields I saw at Passover have changed color. They're as yellow as egg yolk. Not far from the road, I see a large combine harvesting wheat. The grains are left in the combine and the stalks return to the field as bundles of tied hay.

I find Grandma Hannah on the verandah. Grandma is making apricot jam. She washes the orange apricots and places them in a huge pot like a stew pot. She adds sugar, lemons and a fresh vanilla stick with notches in it and the wonderful jam tastes of vanilla. She explains that the apricot season is very short, so she's making a large amount.

Grandpa Yitzhak returns from his errands that afternoon. We visit the cowshed, and then he invites me to sit on the swinging bench under the willow tree.

He looks at me with penetrating eyes, smiles and says: "Well, do you like reading?"

I reply: "Yes, but I prefer listening to stories."

A car enters the yard and Grandpa says: "That's probably Dov."

Dov, Grandpa's brother, lives in Nahariya, about a five minutes' drive from the *Moshav*. Dov is a year older than Grandpa, and he likes to wear a beret.

Grandpa calls out: "Dov, come and sit with us, we have a rather cute guest from Kfar Saba."

Dov sits down beside us and puts a bag of apples next to Grandpa.

Grandma Hannah approaches. She gives us all sweet

cookies and cold tea with slices of lemon, saying to me: "You see these two? They're inseparable. They meet almost every day, or they don't sleep well at night."

I ask: "Grandpa, is that true?"

Grandpa nods: "Very true."

"But why, Grandpa? You're grownups."

Grandpa says: "I don't know, maybe it's because of what we went through when we were children."

"Does it have to do with the war you told me about?"

Grandpa frowns. "It might be, who knows."

I fold my arms and insist: "Won't you tell me about the two of you?"

Grandpa sighs.

"It's hard to talk about the war, much better to forget."

Dov says: "Grandpa's right. Much better to forget."

We're silent.

Dov takes a sip of tea and says: "When we were children we had a good time. We lived in a small village called Tur'i Remety in the Carpathian Mountains in Hungary. There was a large forest near the village. I liked wandering about the forest. I found nuts, mushrooms, raspberry bushes. Most of all I like to climb trees. I'd climb up very fast. When we played hide 'n seek, nobody could find me, because I had a secret hiding place among the branches. In the forest there were wolves and foxes so we always walked there with a stick in our hands, remember, Yitzhak?"

Grandpa Yitzhak says: "I remember, I remember. We also had a river near the village. There were fish in the river. We'd collect worms and throw a line into the river. I don't remember catching anything."

Dov says: "I remember that when we were four, we went to '*cheder*' – the little ones' class. We learned to read Hebrew letters. At home we spoke Yiddish, the language of Jews. We left the house every day at five-thirty. It was dark. In winter, it was 25 degrees below zero, freezing cold. We'd hold hands and walk very slowly. We were afraid of sinking into the snow. We wore a warm vest, a shirt, a sweater and a coat, a hat and scarf, gloves, and two pairs of wool socks. But our faces still hurt, like a burn from boiling water.

We couldn't feel our feet at all because of the cold, and our side curls looked like two pieces of barbed wire. We'd study for two hours and return home. At age six we went to the Gentile primary school. We learned to read and write in Hungarian. We stayed in school until 13:00 and then returned to '*cheder*' for at least two or three more hours."

Grandpa Yitzhak says: "I didn't like going to school. I liked helping father. We had a cowshed in the yard."

I exclaim: "Like the cowshed you have today!"

Grandpa agrees: "Yes, but smaller."

I ask: "And what did you do in your cowshed in Hungary?"

Grandpa says: "I helped my father with the milking, and I went out with the cows to pasture. Other children went out as well. The cows grazed on fresh pasture and we played hide 'n seek, catch, and five stones. But best of all I liked going with father to market. I always found bargains, like a torch or a slingshot, and I also heard stories from shop-owners who'd invite me to sit down."

I jump up: "Gramps, Gramps, can I go out with your cows to pasture?"

Grandpa laughs and says: "Times have changed, my boy, there is no pasture or milking by hand. There are machines instead."

Dov adds: "I liked playing with the Gentile children. Their parents had fields of corn. During the corn-picking season, we'd help them peel the cobs."

"Yes," chimes in Grandpa, "every evening we'd gather at another family's home and when the work was done, we'd sing, dance, and eat hot corn. Until one day…"

Grandpa fell silent.

I say: "Grandpa, go on telling me about your village."

Grandpa sighed. I give him a glass of cold tea and he says: "One day everything came to an end."

I ask: "How old were you?"

Grandpa says: "I was thirteen and Dov was fourteen. The Hungarians forced us to wear a yellow patch on our clothing because we were Jews. All our Hungarian friends distanced themselves from us and we felt very isolated. Some shouted at us 'Jew, get out of here, go to Palestine, that's your home.' I'd beat them up. I didn't tell Mama and Papa."

I ask: "Was it because of the war?"

Grandpa says: "Yes. The Nazis came into power in Germany. They occupied Hungary and turned the Jews out of their homes.

Our family scattered. Some went to a concentration camp, the two of us were sent to a labor camp. I was in Germany, Dov in Poland. We worked very hard in the labor camps, from morning till night. We suffered from cold and starvation, but we never stopped thinking about each other."

I say: "You said you reunited with Dov during the war. How did it happen?"

"Ah, yes," recalls Grandpa. "One day the Germans sent me by train to another labor camp in Germany. In that camp were thousands of prisoners. I walked among the huts, looking for a familiar face. I knew there was no point asking about my family by name because they didn't call us by name. Instead we had numbers written on our clothing. I'm walking along a path next to one of the huts when I suddenly see a boy about my height standing alone. He was very thin and his clothes were dirty. I approached him. He raised his head and looked at me. His face was full of dust, but his eyes were like Dov's eyes. My heart started beating like mad, I said, 'Dov?' and he took a step back, as if he were afraid of me. I leaned forward and said slowly, 'Please answer me, you're Dov?' He didn't speak. I realized that he didn't recognize me because I was also dirty and thin like him. I wet my fingers with saliva and quickly started cleaning my

face. I said, 'Look at me, I'm Yitzhak, Yitzhak, your brother from the village of Tur'i Remety in Hungary, don't you know me?' He looked at me with big eyes and whispered: 'Yitzhak? Yitzhak?'

"We embraced. We couldn't stop crying. I whispered, 'Dov, what have they done to you, I barely recognized you.' Dov whispered 'Yitzhak, Yitzhak, my brother Yitzhak.'

"Suddenly, I see a German guard approaching us. He had a revolver in his belt. He shouted at us: 'What are you two doing here?'

"Holding out my hands, I shouted joyfully: 'I've found my brother! I've found my brother!' I forgot that a Jewish prisoner is forbidden to speak to a German guard. A prisoner who dared speak to a German guard was always punished. The guard gave us an angry look, and left. From that moment on, Dov and I have been inseparable."

Grandpa takes a deep breath and falls silent.

I wait patiently.

Dov sighs and continues instead of Grandpa, "and then we were ordered to leave the camp. It was towards the end of the war. We realized that the Germans were taking all the prisoners on a march. I was too weak to leave, I couldn't go, I was very weak because I'd marched and traveled by train for months from Poland to Germany. I told Yitzhak, 'you go, you have a chance' – but Yitzhak wouldn't hear of it. He said, 'we're together now, Dov, we'll help each other,'

"From that moment we have never been apart. We walked the roads of Germany for almost three months. Our feet hurt. But the hardest thing of all was the hunger. We were given a quarter loaf of bread every two-three days. We received no water. We'd walk with our mouths open in the rain and swallow drops of water. When snow fell, we ate snow.

"One day, we were standing in a large building, waiting in line for bread. We swallowed the bread with one bite and remained hungry. And then I saw I could no longer stand on my feet. Yitzhak looked at me and went to stand in line for a second time. The Germans forbade us to stand in line twice. We were all wearing striped clothing and looked almost the same. This is why they had two dogs who knew how to identify prisoners by smell. I saw Yitzhak approaching the guard who was handing out bread and was very worried. I wanted to shout to him 'come back to me, Yitzhak, come back, the dogs are dangerous' – but I didn't have the strength to shout.

"Yitzhak got to the guard and held out one hand. The guard gave him a piece of bread, but then the dogs smelled him and jumped on him. The guard hit him over the head and he fell to the floor.

"I thought I'd faint with fear. I began to tremble and called to my father in my heart: 'Papa, papa, come and save him, the dogs are killing our Yitzhak, Papaaaaaa!'

"But my brother didn't give up, he fought the dogs and managed to fight them off. And then he jumped up and ran outside. After about a quarter of an hour, he quietly returned to me. His arms were scratched but he took a piece of bread from under his shirt and broke it in two. He gave half to me and took half for himself. I ate the bread and managed to get up again."

Looking at Grandpa Yitzhak, I think to myself, what a hero for a grandfather I have.

Grandpa Yitzhak continues: "The march was hard, but we helped each other. If one of us didn't have the strength to walk, the other would grab the belt of his trousers and help him to go on. Sometimes we couldn't speak we were so weak. We'd stay close to one another, holding hands. And this gave us the strength to continue to walk until the war was over."

I hold out my hands and say, "Gramps, gramps, I want to try something. Let's hold hands."

Grandpa Yitzhak and Dov smile and hold out their hands. We hold hands very tightly and I feel the warmth spreading through my body. We laugh.

Grandpa Yitzhak says quietly, "Sometimes if we feel pain or sadness, a brother or a friend's hand is more important than a bandage on a sore."

Dov smiles: "That's true," and offers Grandpa and me an apple.

We each eat our apples and I say: "I'm glad you found each other and stayed friends."

A VISIT TO POLAND

Grandpa Yitzhak told me many stories. In the meantime, I grew up.

Seven years passed. I'm sixteen and a bit now, and I'm going to visit the concentration camps in Poland with a delegation from my school.

I stand with a *yarmulke – Jewish head-covering for men*, and an Israeli flag spread across my back, and I think about the stories Grandpa Yitzhak told me. We sing the Israeli anthem, standing on Polish ground, and I remember how, years before, Grandpa had sung *'To be a free nation in our country, land of Zion and Jerusalem'*, on Independence Day. I hear sounds of weeping around me. I restrain myself, but feel chills in my body, because I have enormous pride in being part of a free nation. Pride and sadness as well, because my grandfather was a child prisoner here.

I walk through a large, beautiful forest near Tykocin. The guide points to a dirt path and says: "This is where whole families walked, parents, children and grandparents, as if they were on a trip."

Not so! At the end of a trip we return home. They did not.

I walk along the dirt path and hear the rustling of trees, shhh. Shhh. And I know these trees saw it all, but are silent.

Someone asks: "Where was God? How could He have let

this happen?" Tears shine in his eyes.

I hug him and think about my grandfather.

I'm at Auschwitz. Saturday. Hard to speak. I close my eyes and see Grandpa Yitzhak with a small bundle on his back, not even a suitcase to his name. Beside him stands his Mama and Papa, his sister and two brothers, they, too, carrying bundles, and many others like them, from villages and towns in the area, an enormous convoy. And, probably with them were Marishka, Aggie, Yocheved, Leah'leh, Tzili, Meir too, Yaakov, Tuviah, Elisha and Yechezkel, names Grandpa had mentioned. And I think, Grandpa was fifteen and a bit then, a year younger than I, what did he see? What did he feel?

Just at that moment, my telephone vibrates in my pocket. I open it and hear Grandpa's urgent voice, "Ittai, Ittai, how are you, are you all right?"

I hug my telephone and whisper, "I'm all right, Grandpa, I'm all right."

And Grandpa says: "Call me when you leave there, I have to know that you're out of there, call me."

I promise and immediately close my phone because now we're at Birkenau holding a memorial service, lighting candles with '*Kaddish*' and '*Yizkor*' – *a Jewish practice of remembering*. I read an excerpt from a book written about my grandfather, speak the names of my family who did not return from the war. I choke up, my shirt is wet, but my friends hug me, and I know how important and reinforcing it is to stand together. My Grandfather Yitzhak was here alone.

I look at the Auschwitz-Birkenau sky. There is blue, there are clouds, the sun is soft, sometimes overcast, sometimes visible, an ordinary sun, and all I can think is, what color was the sky sixty years ago, when all the things Grandpa told me about took place. What scent was there in the air? Was there a wind, were there birds? Were there flower beds next to the barbed wire fences?

There were no butterflies here, I read about that. Maybe they were alarmed by Nazi screams, or maybe by the blinding lights of the projectors at night. And I know this is why Grandpa can't bear noise, and even worse than that, blinding lights.

I'm home in Israel. I want to thank Grandpa Yitzhak and Grandma Hannah. It was thanks to them that I encountered my roots. I want to tell them: Grandpa, Grandma, you are heroes! I'm proud I participated in the journey to Poland and want to remember everything I felt – pain, tears, occasionally even happiness. But most of all, I want to remember that I am a Jew, the grandson of Holocaust survivors, and privileged to be born and live in a free country.

HOW I WROTE THIS STORY

Ittai is a real boy.

And Grandpa Yitzhak is a real grandfather. All the stories that Grandpa Yitzhak told Ittai are true stories.

And I know them – Grandpa Yitzhak, Grandma Hannah, and Ittai.

I was a baby when Yitzhak came to our home. He was seventeen and a bit.

At the end of the Second World War, youngsters who'd lost their family in the Holocaust emigrated to Israel. A group of 25 boys and girls came to my village. They were known as the 'Holocaust survivor group from Poland'. Among them were the brothers, Yitzhak and Dov.

They were distributed among the families in the village, went to school and worked. Yitzhak was invited to eat a daily lunch in my parents' home. Dov was invited to eat at another house. The group didn't assimilate in the village and, within two years, they'd all left.

Yitzhak kept in touch with my parents over the years, I saw him as an adopted brother. He visited us in the village and we always celebrated family events together.

When I was a young girl, I asked my mother: "Where does Yitzhak come from? Why doesn't he have parents?" Mother told me: "He comes from *there*. Shhh…we don't talk about it."

I asked no more questions but I was curious.

Years went by. I visited Yitzhak at his home. I asked him to tell me what he went through during the war. He refused to speak, merely saying: "I experienced hard things, better to forget."

More years went by.

After I submitted my first manuscript to Prosa Publications, a book for adults called **Come Auntie, Let's Dance**, I knew in my heart that the next book would be Yitzhak and Dov's story. I met Dov at Yitzhak's family events. I told Dror, my husband, that my next book will be about Yitzhak and Dov.

He laughed and said: "What do you mean, they refuse to talk!"

I replied: "That's what I feel. They don't know it yet."

I traveled to meet with Yitzhak and Dov. Dov lives with his family in Nahariya, Yitzhak lives with his family on a *Moshav*

nearby. I asked them to tell me about *their* Holocaust, but they refused. I compromised. "Are you willing to tell me about the days after you reached Israel?" To this, they agreed.

And that's how it began.

For a year, I traveled by train to Nahariya.

I sat with them for several hours at a time, sometimes together, sometimes apart. They spoke and I wrote. I also recorded them just to be sure.

After a year, their story was on my computer. It took me another two years to turn their personal story into a book.

During this period, I read many books about the Holocaust. When I finished writing the book, I went to Poland.

As Holocaust Day 2004 in Israel approached, the book for adults that I'd written about them, Icho and Bernard, was published. These were Dov and Yitzhak's names in Hungary.

Then the idea of writing about Dov and Yitzhak for children came about. I drew on details from Icho and Bernard and that's how this book, My Grandfather and his Mysterious Friend, was born.

A few months ago, Ittai, Yitzhak's grandson, went with a school delegation to visit Poland. He returned greatly moved by the journey and wrote wonderful things. Some of what he wrote appears in the previous chapter you read in this book, "A Visit to Poland."

I wish to thank Grandpa Yitzhak and Grandma Hannah, Grandpa Dov and Grandma Shosh, their sons and daughters, and their grandchildren, particularly Ittai, who shared his personal and touching writing with me.

Also, thanks to Grandma Sida and her granddaughter, Tamar. Today, Tamar is my daughter-in-law. My thanks also to Anat Raz, from Prosa Publications who suggested this children's book.

I am not a second-generation Holocaust survivor. My parents emigrated from Bulgaria to Israel in 1935.

They were pioneers and established the first 'Wall and Tower' settlement, Kfar Hittim, in the Lower Galilee overlooking the Sea of Galilee. My family did not go through the Holocaust, but as an Israeli Jewess, I felt a need to write a book about this terrible chapter of our nation's history. My relationship with Yitzhak and Dov enabled me to set out on this journey.

I hope this story inspires your interest.

I believe we all have an obligation to remember, and never, ever forget.

Thank you,
Malka Adler

www.ingramcontent.com/pod-product-compliance
Lightning Source LLC
LaVergne TN
LVHW091539070526
838199LV00002B/124